RICKIE

By Mary Octavia Davis · Illustrated by Dutz

Steck-Vaughn Company   •   Austin, Texas

To
My brother and sisters

Francis Marion Davis

Anne Elizabeth Davis

Lucy Justine Davis

Elvira Rothe Davis

LIBRARY OF CONGRESS

CATALOG CARD NUMBER 55-7878

Rickie was a little rooster. He lived
in the country.

He had a beautiful tail. It curled up
instead of down.

Everybody said, "What a beautiful tail!"
This made Rickie the rooster very proud.

It made him too proud. He thought he was
a big rooster.

8

The old hens shook their heads and said,
"Cluck, cluck, cluck. He thinks he is the cock
of the walk."

Rickie pranced around eating everything. Bugs
and beetles! Bees and butterflies! Worms and
ants! Everything!

His mother said, "For shame, Rickie, to eat everything in sight!"

But Rickie would not listen to her. He kept on eating.

He ate the kitten's dinner.

He ate the duck's dinner.

He ate the parrot's dinner.

He ate the pig's dinner.

He ate the baby chick's dinner.

He ate the pigeon's dinner.

13

Soon nobody wanted to be around Rickie
because he was so greedy. They all ran away
when they saw him coming.

But Rickie didn't care. He was too busy eating and eating and eating.

He was so busy eating that he did not notice
what was happening to him.

Do you know what it was?
He was getting bigger and BIGGER and BIGGER!

Soon Rickie was so big that he could hardly
walk.

And then one day his beautiful tail suddenly
straightened out!

18

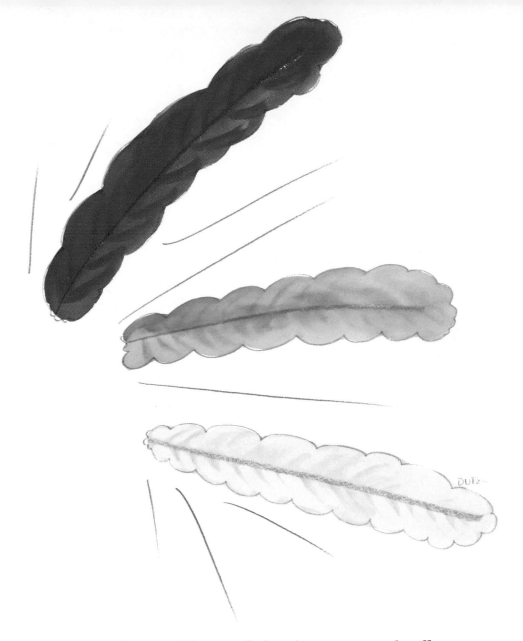

Ping! The red feather popped off.
Pang! The green feather popped off.
Pong! The yellow feather popped off.

And there stood Rickie like a big round ball, with no tail at all.

"Oh, oh!" he cried. "I've lost my tail, my beautiful tail."

Then he ran off and hid where he thought nobody could see him. He was so ashamed.

But his mother found him. "Cluck, cluck," she said gently. "My poor greedy little rooster."

"I want my beautiful tail back," Rickie cried. "I want my friends, too. What can I do?"

His mother said, "You must be good and kind. You must not be greedy. You must let others have their share of food, too."

This was very hard for Rickie to do. He still wanted to eat everything in sight. But he kept on trying and trying.

He waited for the
kitten to eat.

He waited for the
duck to eat.

He waited for the
parrot to eat.

He waited for the
pig to eat.

He waited for the
baby chick to eat.

He waited for the
pigeon to eat.

He let everyone else eat first. He was so kind
and polite that his friends did not run away
any more.

Rickie even forgot he had no tail at all.

Then one day the little duck quacked, "Rickie, Rickie! Look! Your tail is growing out again."

27

He looked. His tail was growing out again!
But now it turned DOWN instead of UP.

And do you know what?
Ever since that time all roosters are happy to let the hens and chicks eat first.

And all their beautiful tails turn down
instead of up!

And Rickie is truly the cock of the walk!